THIS BOOK BELONGS TO

....

....

HEY
DUGGEE

LADYBIRD BOOKS

UK | USA | Canada | Ireland | Australia | India | New Zealand | South Africa

Ladybird Books is part of the Penguin Random House group of companies
whose addresses can be found at global.penguinrandomhouse.com.

www.penguin.co.uk   www.puffin.co.uk   www.ladybird.co.uk

Penguin
Random House
UK

First published 2020
002

Text and illustrations copyright © Studio AKA Limited, 2020
Adapted by Lauren Holowaty

Printed in China

A CIP catalogue record for this book is available from the British Library

ISBN: 978-1-405-94296-6

All correspondence to:
Ladybird Books
Penguin Random House Children's
One Embassy Gardens, New Union Square
5 Nine Elms Lane, London SW8 5DA

HEY DUGGEE

DUGGEE'S PARTY!

NORRIE   TAG   DUGGEE   BETTY   ROLY   HAPPY

Duggee is busy building a model when the clubhouse doorbell rings . . .

DING - DONG!

"*There's somebody at the door!*" sing the Squirrels.
They race off to find out who it is . . .

It's Delivery Chipmunk with a parcel for Duggee!

"I wonder what's inside," says Betty.
"It's wrapped up like a present," says Roly.
Happy gasps. "It must be Duggee's birthday!"
"Yeah!" everyone agrees.

"We should have a surprise party
for Duggee!" cries Tag.
"What do we need?" asks Betty.

"Duggee will know," says Norrie. "He has his **Party Badge!**"

The Squirrels rush over to Duggee ...

"WAIT!"

calls Tag, stopping everyone in their tracks. "We can't ask Duggee. If we do, his party won't be a surprise! We'll have to . . . **DO IT OURSELVES!**"

The Squirrels' jaws drop. Duggee always helps them!

Roly looks for the party balloons, but he can't find them anywhere.

DUGGEE, WHERE ARE THE BALLOONS?

"Woof woof woof!" replies Duggee. "In the balloon box," says Roly. "Of course!" Then he whispers to Duggee, "We're not doing you a party!" and runs off.

Roly pumps up lots and lots and LOTS of balloons.

Soon, the whole clubhouse is full of party balloons!

"I think that's enough balloons now, Roly!" cries Betty.

Norrie and Happy want to
make paper-chain decorations.
But they need a little help from ...

DUGGEE!

SNIP, SNIP, SNIP!

Duggee is good at making paper chains. "Ah-woof!" says Duggee.

THANKS, DUGGEE!

Betty and Tag decide who to invite to the party. "Enid, Frog . . ."

They make some colourful invitations.

"INVITATIONS READY!"

they cry, running off to deliver them . . .

"Come to Duggee's surprise party," say Betty and Tag, hand-delivering each invitation.

Balloons done.

Decorations done.

Invitations done.

WHAT'S NEXT?

"**Birthday cake!**" cheer the Squirrels, jumping up and down.

"Bread, raisins – cake made!" says Betty.
"Let's decorate it with everything Duggee likes . . ."
"Custard and spaghetti," says Tag, adding dry spaghetti strands to the cake.
"Lettuce and sprinkles!" adds Happy.

Soon after, the guests arrive,
and the Squirrels call Duggee over.

"SURPRISE! HAPPY BIRTHDAY, DUGGEE!"

"Uhhh-woof?" says Duggee, surprised and confused.
"It's not your birthday?" asks Norrie. "But we saw
Delivery Chipmunk bring you a present!"
Duggee shakes his head and opens the parcel . . .

Betty

. . . Inside are little figures for Duggee's model! Happy gasps. "Look! Duggee's model is all of us in the clubhouse!"

"They're having a party!" cries Norrie.
"And so are we!" adds Betty, giggling.

"Time for cake!" cries Tag excitedly.
Duggee's surprise cake looks amazing,
and everyone tucks in . . .

"EURGHH!"

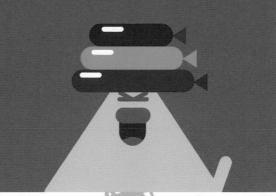

Duggee's surprise cake
doesn't taste amazing.
Never mind, the party
is still lots of fun!

Haven't the Squirrels done well today, Duggee? They have definitely earned their Party Badges.

AH-WOOF!

Now there's just time for one more
thing before the Squirrels go home . . .